Kids learn so much
Adventures

Written by **Kandace Caine**

3D Renderings by
Aspak Mansuri

Illustrations by
Willie Carwell

"Kids Learn So Much Adventures"

Watch
LIKE   COMMENT SUBSCRIBE

 facebook.com/kidslearnsomuch

 YouTube

 IG: @kidslearnsomuch
IG: @kandacecaine_

(Subscribe FREE)
youtube.com/c/KidsLearnSoMuch

Check back regularly for new episodes.

www.kidslearnsomuch.com

KIDS LEARN SO MUCH Copyright 2020 Kandace Caine
ISBN 978-1-7355106-0-6

1

Introduction Page

I try and write from my heart. I have had the pleasure of teaching children from all over the world. I love to write fun stories based on children getting into mischief and having fun adventures. Kids Learn So Much was created first as a TV show to help teach children Science, Technology, Engineering, Arts and Math (STEAM), as well as Arts & Crafts, Singing, Languages, Acting and Puppetry. Now, *Kids Learn So Much Adventures* has been turned into an animation series for children to escape into a magical world with Amara, Kehinde, Michael, Wang Yong, Olivia and Ms. Gold. I was inspired to write it during the Covid-19 pandemic which made a lot of changes for children around the world in the year 2020. You can watch the show on You Tube under: *youtube.com/c/KidsLearnSoMuch.* I hope that you have enjoyed these stories as much as I have enjoyed writing them.

Contents

Thank You's

I want to first thank my parents. They pushed me to be as creative as I possibly could be. Without their support I could not have accomplished all that I have. I want to thank my family and friends for always believing in my vision. I want to thank everyone who has supported me along my journey. Manu & Sheila you are my world and I thank you from the bottom of my heart. I want to thank Willie Carwell, my incredible illustrator for always being so positive and supportive. Aspak Mansuri for his incredible work on the animated show. I want to thank Olivia Roberts for all of her support editing everything. I also want to thank Jason Sims for book layout. Last but not least I want to thank all of the children that I have had the pleasure of teaching. You inspire me and helped me get to this point! Thank You!

Meet the Characters

Ms. Gold   (29 years old) British. Is a strict, lovable, but goofy teacher. She believes in education and children having fun whilst learning. She will get the children out of any situation no matter how difficult it is.

Kehinde   (16 years old): West-African. A Twin. Nerdy, organized, and efficient. She is an expert in computer games and comic books. Loves pizza.

Michael (16 years old): Afro-American. He is loving, extremely kind, loud, thinks he is always right. Great at art. Lactose intolerant. Hates Pizza.

王勇 **Wang Yong**   (16 years old): English-Northern. He loves to sing and is good at it. He is also a mathematician. He wears glasses and some would call him a genius.

Amara (16 years old): Takes her time with things, smart, a comedian, a risk taker. Born in New Delhi in India, but moved to Los Angeles when she was 13 years old. She is a great storyteller and will either be a comedian or an activist when she grows up or both.

Olivia   (16 years old) A Valley Girl. Californian. Bossy, a straight talker, loves social media, loves to read romantic books, spoiled. She plays the flute.

Abducted by Aliens

THE GOLDEN ACADEMY

Inside The Golden Academy, **Ms. Gold** stands in front of five students who are sitting on chairs in their classroom facing Ms. Gold.

Michael, Kehinde, Amara, and **Olivia** stare at Ms. Gold. **Wang Yong** (looks at his phone).

Ms. Gold doesn't look happy.

MS. GOLD

Good Morning class. As you can see Mr. Haddad has not turned up to work today along with the other teachers at this school and students because of the Coronavirus.

So it is just us in school today. It seems as though today will be the last day we are open as we will have to close and follow the Center for Disease Control's guidelines. It is serious so it is important that you all wash your hands and...

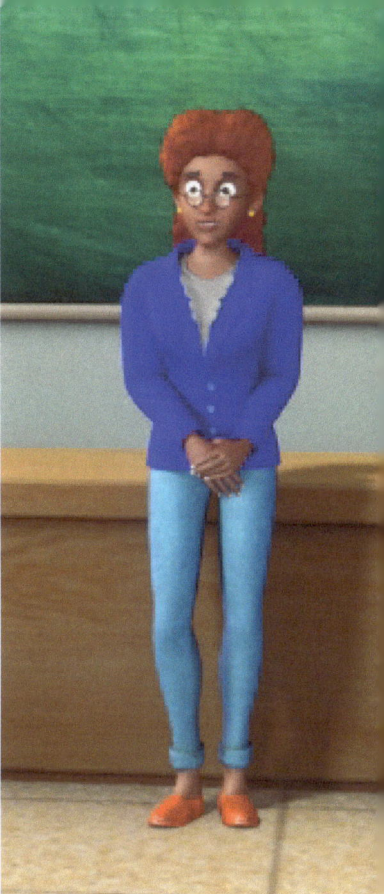

Michael gets up from his seat and holds up his phone and plays music. He begins to dance to the music.

MICHAEL

And have some fun Ms. Gold.

If we are the only kids in school then learning anything today doesn't make sense. We should have fun. How about doing a party live on Instagram like DJ D- Nice did last week!

WANG YONG

DJ D-Nice on Instagram, are you kidding me, he is old! Michael we all know that having a party when there is a pandemic doesn't actually make sense.

MICHAEL

A pan what?

AMARA

A pandemic is a global outbreak of a disease that is deadly and kills.

MS. GOLD

Michael turn off that music NOW !!
Michael turns the music off on his phone immediately.

OLIVIA

We need to all calm down. No one is going to die, ok, ok. Corona is actually an epidemic not a pandemic.

WANG YONG

Why do your parents actually pay for you to come to this school? People are dying everyday Olivia, do you watch the news? Do you think the school would be closing if only California had it. This is a global thing, a pandemic!

OLIVIA

You need to lower your voice Wang Yong, ok, ok! Just because you were born in England that does not make you a genius, ok, ok. You are not royalty Wang Yong, leave that to Prince Harry.

KEHINDE

All of you'll need to shut up. Seriously. First of all, we all know Prince Harry ain't no prince no more, and second of all, Olivia, this is bigger than an epidemic and Wang Yong if you know all of this how come you at school today?

WANG YONG

Because my parents are still visiting family in England and my auntie who is looking after me doesn't really like me, so she said it's best I go to school today.

OLIVIA

She doesn't like you! I wonder why!

The lights turn off and all you see in the dark are green flashing lights, like lights from outer space making buzzing sounds.

MS. GOLD
What what was that?

MICHAEL
What the heck!

AMARA
The lights have gone off!

KEHINDE
I'm go switch the lights

back on simples!
Kehinde tries to switch on the light but it doesn't come on.

A blue beast-like creature is standing in front of Ms. Gold, leaving Olivia, Wang Yong, Michael, Kehinde and Amara speechless and just starring at the beast.

(The beast roars)

MS. GOLD
Please don't hurt us!

The monster roars at Ms. Gold.

Ms. Gold and the kids run off and the monster follows them.

WANG YONG
What was that thing?

Hours later. The kids return to their classroom. Ms. Golds is back in the classroom. She stands holding a picture of a Red Time Machine that is on her wall.

MS.GOLD

Listen Kids! If that beast turns up again. I want you to touch this picture and say its name three times, but only if the beast turns up.

WANG YONG

What is its name Ms. Gold?

MS.GOLD

Fabulous Invention!

AMARA

Fabulous Invention?

MS. GOLD

Do not say it again Amara!
The lights turn on and off and the Blue Beast is standing behind them
roaring.

EVERYONE

Fabulous Invention, Fabulous Invention, Fabulous Invention.
Olivia touches the picture and the Time Machine comes out of the
picture and is right in front of them.

Episode 2
Planet Corona

(We begin the story with the entrance of the Time Machine in the middle of nowhere on a creepy planet with nothing but glowing blue eggs surrounding the Time Machine.)

(We soon cut to all 5 teenagers and Ms. Gold falling out of the Time Machine onto the black surface of Planet Corona and the time machine going back into Ms. Gold's picture that she is holding in her hand.)

AMARA
The Time Machine worked Ms. Gold! How did you get it?

KEHINDE
Amara! The question you should be asking is where are we and is this still planet Earth?

WANG YONG
This is not Earth.

OLIVIA
And how do you know that Wang Yong! We are breathing right now without a helmet, of course we are still on Earth.

Michael stands there shaking in shock as they all speak.

MS. GOLD
All of you be quiet. This doesn't feel or look like anywhere I have been before, so we need to be quiet as we could have enemies.

MICHAEL
That is true Ms. Gold. Why are there so many Blue Eggs? They could be Aliens!!!

KEHINDE
Which is why Ms. Gold said be quiet fool.

AMARA
Maybe we should try and go back into the picture and call the time machine's name?

MICHAEL
That is a great idea!!

Ms. Gold then puts the picture on the ground and puts her hand on the picture.

OLIVIA
I think we should explore this place and look around. It's cool. I have never seen blue eggs, ok, ok. They are awesome.

Olivia is laughing to herself and starts to walk around the eggs. She picks one up and throws it up in the air. The egg falls to the floor and cracks open.

WANG YONG
The eggs are cracking open because of you Olivia. You're crazy! What have you done Olivia? Ms. Gold we have to get back in the machine as we don't know if the eggs are deadly.

Olivia picks up one of the eggs.

OLIVIA
They have green slime. Gross!

One of the blue eggs cracks and this time a blue hand comes out of the egg, then a foot, then two heads pop out. This tall creature just stands looking at Ms. Gold, Olivia, Wang Yong, Michael, Kehinde, and Amara, leaving them speechless and staring at the blue creature. The creature walks towards them. There is some distance between him and the children.

Wang Yong quickly puts his hand on the picture.

WANG YONG
I have to get us out of this mess! Fabulous Invention, Fabulous Invention, Fabulous Invention.

As Wang Yong puts his hand on the picture it becomes big again and the Time Machine is standing yet again in the middle of all of these cracked blue eggs.

Ms. Gold, Olivia, Wang Yong, Michael, Kehinde, and Amara all run inside the Time Machine followed by the blue creature. The Time Machine disappears.

End of Episode 2

Episode 3
Pluto

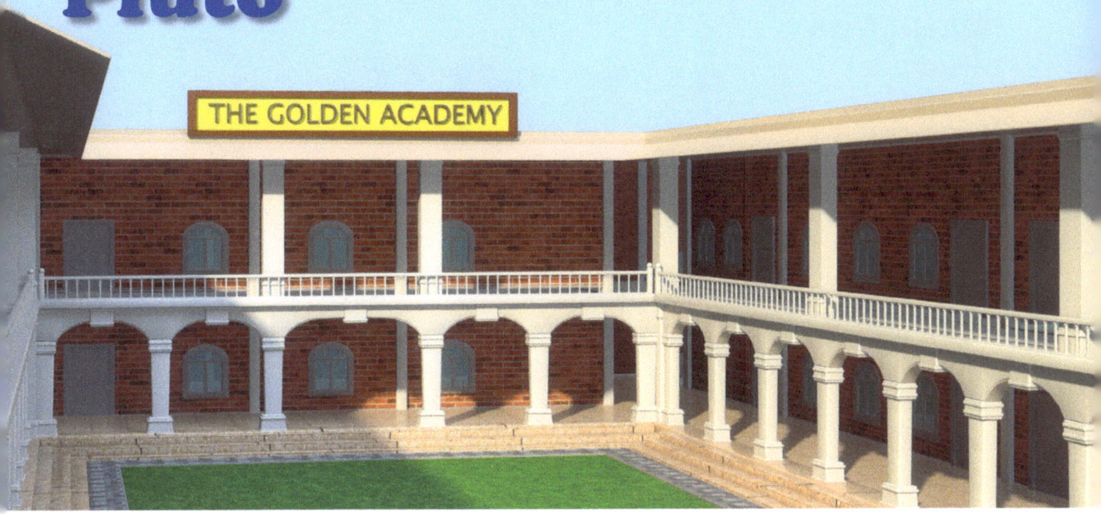

THE GOLDEN ACADEMY

The group returns to The Golden Academy.

The Time Machine is in the middle of the room. The children and Ms. Gold come out with the monster.

All of the children rush to hide in the classroom. Ms. Gold stands up holding the monster in her hand. Michael, Kehinde, Wang Yong, Amara, and Olivia stare at Ms. Gold shocked.

MS. GOLD
Children come out and stop hiding. I have this all under control. This Blue Boy is not going to hurt you.

The monster makes funny sounds. He is communicating but the children and Ms. Gold do not understand him. Olivia understands him.

OLIVIA

He is saying put him down because you are hurting him Ms. Gold!

WANG YONG

What, you can speak an alien language now Olivia!

MS. GOLD

He could run away Olivia. We need to keep him in this room. He needs to go back in the time machine.

AMARA

But how do you know that the next place the time machine goes to will be it's planet?

OLIVIA

We will have to take that risk Amara. Everyone, he is called Pluto and he is only a baby. He wants to go back to his planet. He needs food.

MICHAEL

I ain't going back in that machine. Oh no! Tell Pluto NO WAY!

KEHINDE

Shhh everyone. Seriously. I will go back and take him. I have faith that I will get there safely and return home.

MS. GOLD

You are all going home Kehinde. I am calling your parents and they are going to collect you. We must not discuss any of this with them. Today has been very hectic and we are lucky to be back here. I will return Pluto to his home. Olivia how can you understand him?

WANG YONG

Ms. Gold we have to come with you. How did you find this time machine?

MS.GOLD

My father gave me the painting. He said that it is a very important picture that I should always look after.

OLIVIA

I understand Pluto because I think he is communicating through me.

MS. GOLD

Olivia how do you know this?

The blue monster jumps out of Ms.Gold's hand and runs to Olivia! It whispers in her ear.

OLIVIA

Pluto has to go back to his planet or he will die!!

Olivia runs to the time machine and opens the door and goes inside with the monster. The time machine vanishes. Kehinde, Michael, Wang Yong, Amara and Ms. Gold are speechless.

End of Episode 3

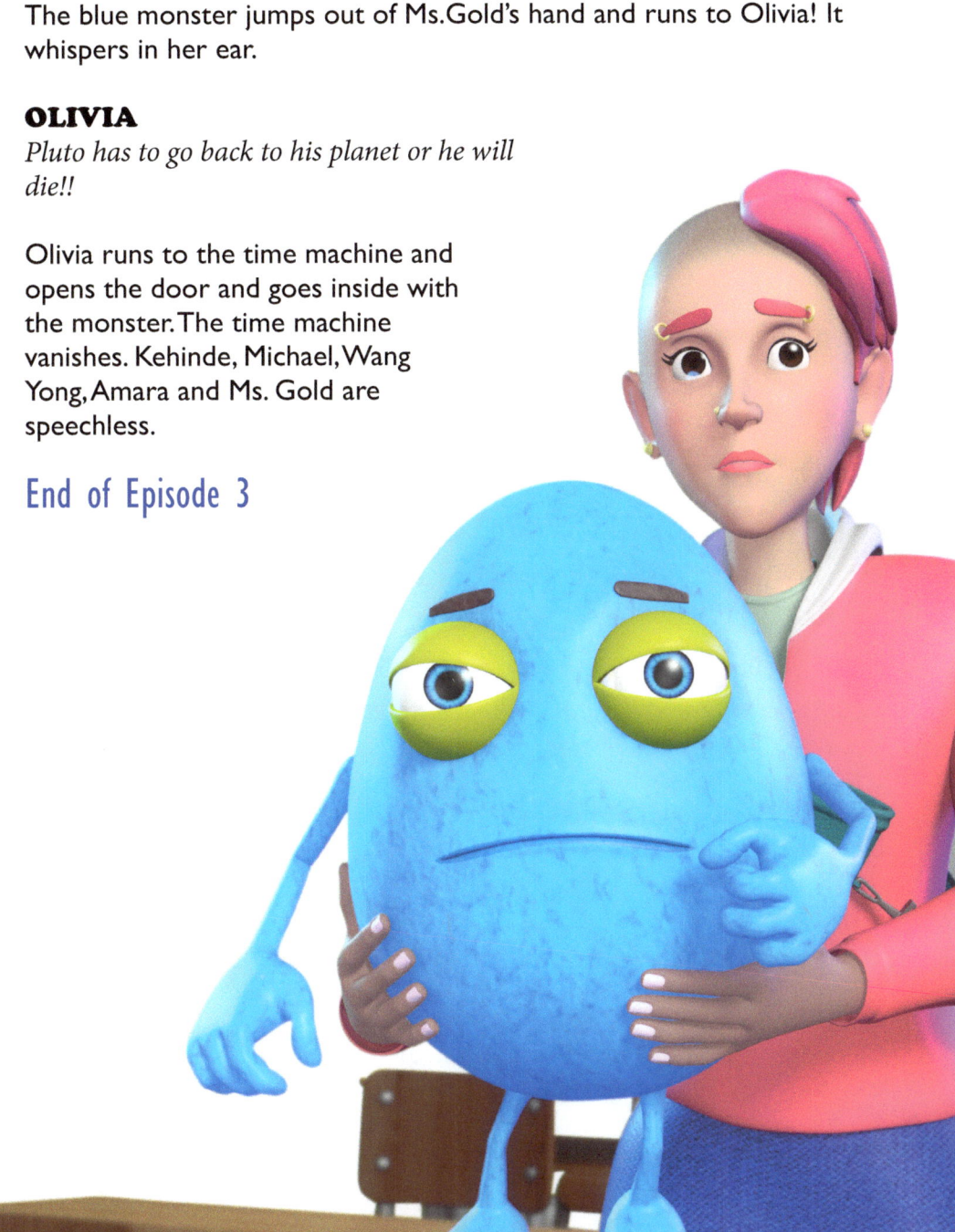

Episode 4
Olivia

Back on Planet Corona. The entrance of the Time Machine is in the middle of nowhere on a creepy planet with nothing but glowing blue eggs surrounding the Time Machine.

Olivia comes out of the time machine holding Pluto close to her chest. She walks around the planet trying not to step on the eggs.

She puts Pluto down. Pluto smiles at her and runs off. She chases after him but he disappears.

OLIVIA
Why are you running Pluto. Don't you want to say goodbye? I have to get back home Pluto.

Olivia turns around and walks back to the time machine. She is about to walk into the time machine when she hears Pluto scream.

PLUTO
NOOOOOOOOO. You are not allowed to go back.

OLIVIA

You can speak English Pluto? And why are you saying I can't go back home?

PLUTO

You must stay here. You will be my wife.

OLIVIA

You're kidding me right? Your wife! I helped you Pluto and for that you want me to marry you? No!

Four other blue aliens that look exactly like Pluto come out of nowhere walking towards Olivia. They are holding a blue egg. They give the egg to Olivia. Olivia pushes the egg away.

OLIVIA

You are all creeping me out. I am going home.

All of the aliens jump on Olivia and she falls to the floor. She manages to push them off her and run back inside the time machine. The time machine disappears.

Back inside Mr. Haddad's classroom, Ms. Gold stands looking worried next to Michael, Kehinde, Wang Yong (who is looking at his phone) and Amara. Ms. Gold doesn't look happy until she sees the time machine.

Olivia runs out and they all run to her and hug her.

OLIVIA
I never thought I would say this but I am glad to be back at school with all of you. Pluto tried to marry me! He wouldn't let me leave his planet.

WANG YONG
Marry you!

OLIVIA
Yes marry me. I had to fight them off me. I ran into the time machine and came back here.
They all continue to hug Olivia and Ms. Gold just smiles.

End of Episode 4

KIDS LEARN SO MUCH MUCH ADVENTURES

Lightsaber

Inside Mr. Haddad's classroom, the Time Machine is still in the middle of the room. Amara, Wang Yong, Kehinde, and Michael are sitting down at their desks listening to Olivia tell them about what happened whilst she was on the planet with Pluto.

OLIVIA

They were so creepy!

MS. GOLD

Shhh Olivia. I can hear something coming from the time machine.

Ms. Gold walks over to the time machine and opens the door. Out pops Pluto with three more aliens that look exactly like him. They are all holding lightsaber swords. They point them at Ms. Gold, Amara, Kehinde, Michael, Wang Yong, and Olivia who are shocked.

OLIVIA

This doesn't make any sense. I left the planet and they were not in the time machine.

PLUTO

Shut up little girl

OLIVIA

Don't you tell me to shut up. And who are you are calling me little? I should knock your-

PLUTO

We will use these weapons on your friends if you say another word Olivia!

Wang Yong jumps on Pluto and grabs the lightsaber sword but Pluto's friends end up hitting Wang Yong on the head with their lightsaber and he falls down to the ground. Pluto takes back the lightsaber from Wang Yong. Wang Yong is on the floor unconscious. Pluto looks at Olivia and points the lightsaber sword at her.

PLUTO

You will marry me! You will marry me on my planet Corona or you will all face the consequences.

MS. GOLD

Pluto! Olivia is just a child. She can not marry you. Please put the sword down.

Pluto points the lightsaber sword at Ms. Gold, Amara, Kehinde, and Michael. As all the aliens point their lightsaber swords at them they all fall to the floor as though the swords are hypnotizing them.

OLIVIA

Let them go Pluto. It is me that you want.

PLUTO

You will marry me and come back to my planet Corona where you will live for the rest of your life.

OLIVIA

I have to speak to my parents Pluto. I have to let them know that I will be marrying you. I have to phone them.

PLUTO

You will leave with me now Olivia, with your family, as they will be at the wedding.

Olivia points to her friends and Ms. Gold.

OLIVIA

They are not my family Pluto, they are my friends from school. Please don't do this.

Pluto then points the lightsaber sword at them and gestures for them to go inside the time machine along with Olivia. They all get up and walk to the time machine. As they go into the time machine Michael whispers to Kehinde.

MICHAEL

(quietly)
We need to get those lightsaber swords from them. Those swords are really powerful.

They are all now in the time machine and the time machine disappears.

End of Episode 5

Episode 6
Marriage

We are back on Planet Corona. Pluto's planet. The Time Machine is in the middle of the creepy planet with nothing but glowing blue eggs surrounding the Time Machine yet again.

Pluto comes out of the time machine with the other aliens who are holding their lightsaber swords and pointing them at Amara, Michael, Kehinde, Olivia, Wang Yong, and Ms. Gold.

Pluto and the other aliens look at Amara and Kehinde. They start to whisper to each other.

Amara, Kehinde, Michael, Wang Yong, Ms. Gold, and Olivia stand together. Amara whispers to Kehinde.

AMARA
I don't like the way they just looked at us.

KEHINDE
It is like they are making plans for us!

MICHAEL
We need to take the lightsaber swords from them. The swords are making them strong.

WANG YONG
I tried that Michael and it didn't work out. What do you suggest we do?

MS. GOLD
Show them your phone Michael. Distract them. Then we must all rush to get the swords. Show them something clever on your phone. Do it now.

Michael walks over to them and starts to show them his phone. He points to the screen and shows them how it works.

Both of the blue aliens put down their lightsaber swords so that they can focus on the Wang Yong's phone. Kehinde and Amara run to pick up the swords. Kehinde and Amara then point their swords at them.

KIDS LEARN SO MUCH MUCH ADVENTURES

As they point the swords at the two aliens, the aliens shrink and become liquid, like a pool of water. Pluto gets so angry that he starts to run around the planet, picking up the eggs and smashing them on the floor. He holds his lightsaber sword and points it at Olivia. He hits her arm with it and she falls to the floor in a deep sleep. Ms. Gold goes to pick her up with Amara and Kehinde.

MS.GOLD
We need to get back into the time machine. Olivia is hurt. Quickly let us all go to it now.

WANG YONG
I will fight off Pluto.

MICHAEL

I will help you.

Amara, Kehinde, and Ms. Gold are holding Olivia who is unconscious and they go into the time machine. Wang Yong is pushing off Pluto who is trying to get into the time machine. Michael grabs Pluto's sword and gives him a firm push. They then run into the time machine and it disappears leaving Pluto behind screaming on planet Corona.

PLUTO

Ahhhhhh. COME BACK OLIVIA. MY WIFE!!!! Come back!!!!!

End of Episode 6

Episode 7
Egypt - An Eye For An Eye

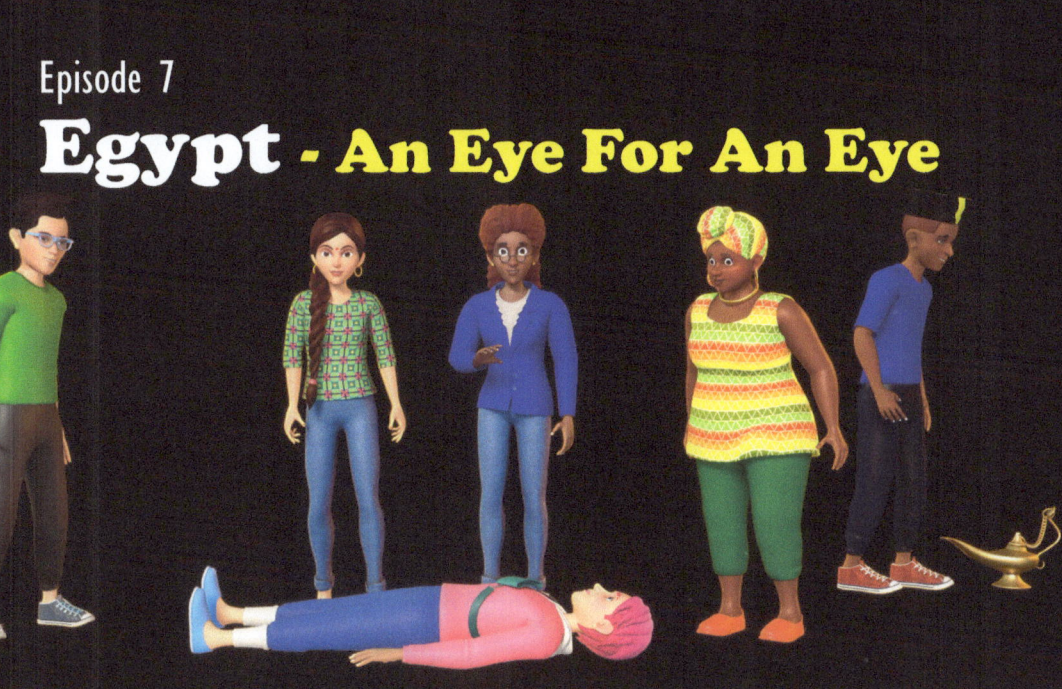

(We begin the story with the entrance of The Egyptian Pyramids.)
(We soon cut to an Egyptian tomb and the Time Machine in the middle of the room next to a golden lamp.)

Wang Yong, Michael, Ms. Gold, Amara, and Kehinde are holding Olivia as they come out of the Time Machine. They place her on the floor. Ms. Gold is holding the lightsaber sword but puts it on the floor. They all look shocked at where they have ended up. Amara falls to the floor and starts to cry. As she cries Ms. Gold walks over to Olivia and puts her arm around Amara and they all just stare at Olivia.

AMARA
Where are we?

MS. GOLD
We are in Egypt. We are in one of the ancient tombs. We need to find water to give to Olivia and get back in the time machine and go home.

Ms. Gold puts her hand on Olivia's shoulder.

WANG YONG
Olivia is alive, but unconscious.

KEHINDE

It is like Pluto put a spell on her.

MICHAEL

Spells are not real Kehinde.

MS. GOLD

Stop this arguing. Right now I need you all to look around this room for water. Olivia needs water.

Amara, Kehinde, Michael and Wang Yong look around the room for water. Michael picks up the golden lamp.

MICHAEL

I found a golden lamp guys. I'm gonna make a wish that Olivia wakes up!

KEHINDE

So you do not believe in spells, Michael, but you believe you can rub the golden lamp and your wish will come true?

WANG YONG

Stay focused, you two! We need to find water, not a lamp or anything else, but water. We need to get back in the time machine and get Olivia help. This is serious!

MS. GOLD

Olivia is awake!

AMARA

Looks like you got your wish Michael. Olivia is awake.

As soon as Amara says this the lights go off and then come back on and standing by Michael's side is a scary mummy.

Michael screams and runs over to Ms. Gold. He is holding the golden lamp. The Mummy walks towards Michael.

MUMMY

Your wish is my command young boy.

MICHAEL

What!

MUMMY

You wished for her to be awake and she is now awake! Now you must come with me young boy!

The mummy grabs Michael and walks away with him. Wang Yong, Amara, and Kehinde all jump on the mummy. Ms. Gold picks up the lightsaber sword and points it at the mummy.

MS. GOLD

I need you to put him down now!!! This sword is strong enough to destroy you. Put him down!!!

MUMMY

An eye for an eye Ms. Gold! If you do not let me take him, Olivia will fall back into a deep sleep and when she awakes, she will never be the same again!! The choice is yours.

End of Episode 7

KIDS LEARN SO MUCH MUCH ADVENTURES

www.ingramcontent.com/pod-product-compliance
Lightning Source LLC
Chambersburg PA
CBHW041031170626
46815CB00001B/50